THE SLIMY BOOK

Babette Cole

PictureLions

An Imprint of HarperCollinsPublishers

Sticky, sludgy, slippy slime,

the sloppy, ploppy, creepy kind.

Slime in
my
pocket,

in my
shoe.

Is it
custard?

Is it glue?

Hello, slimy squids,

slugs,

snails,

and
slippery
toads
in slimy
pails.

Slimy worms on the lawn,

newts
from
ponds,

and green
frog-spawn.

Octopi
with slimy
limbs

eat little fish with slimy fins!

Fat ladies rub slime on their skin,

hoping it will make them thin!

People with no teeth, it's said,

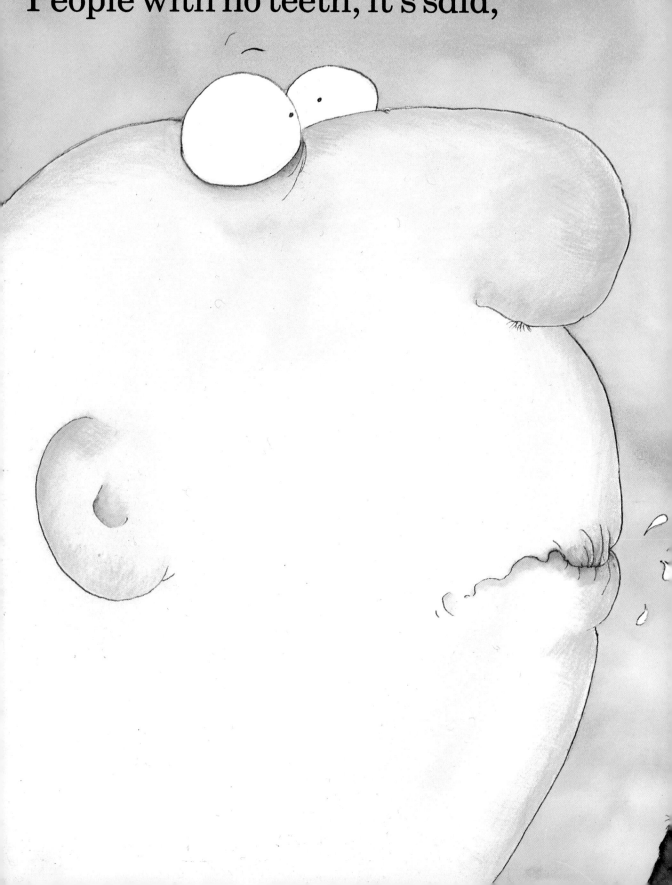

can't eat a slimy pickled egg!

Slime loves dribbling down the drain,
and blocking all the pipes again!

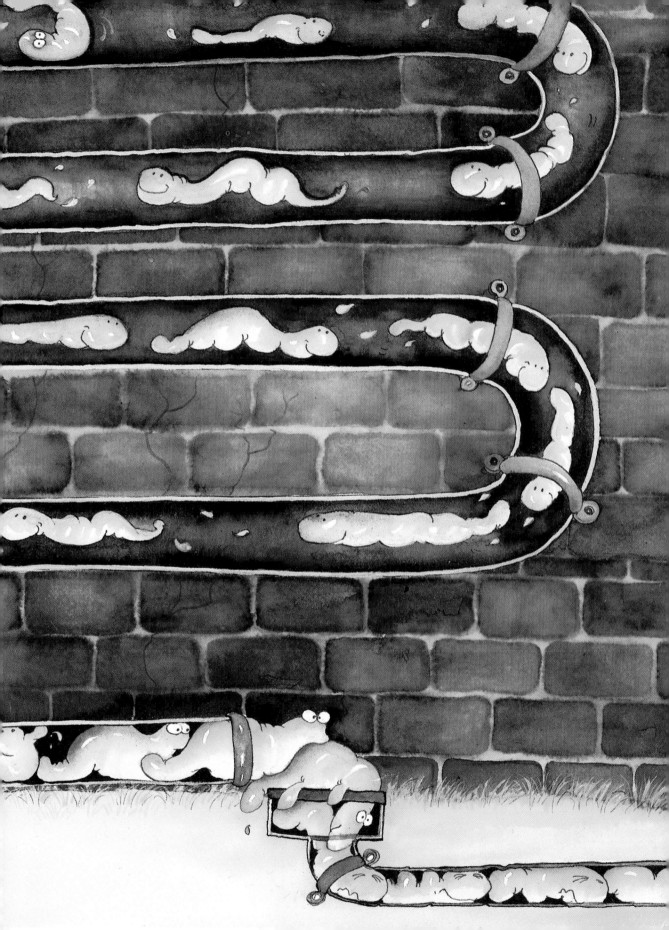

I wonder how it really feels,
slurping slimy
jellied eels…

Here's someone having slime for tea,
I hope they never invite me!

Blimey! Slimy, oodles noodles,

slimy sausages for poodles…

Slimy butter,

slimy jelly,

slimy baked beans,

bulging belly!

I should have listened
to my Mum,

And I wish
I hadn't tried
those horrid sweets
with slime inside!

With all the slime inside this book,
strange creatures came to have a look,

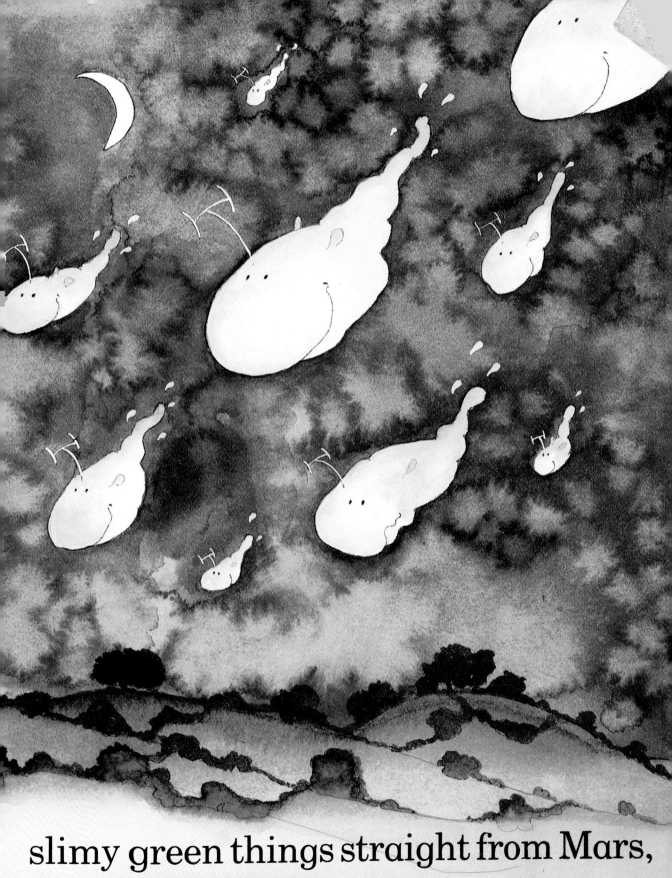

slimy green things straight from Mars,
and planets far beyond the stars,

they ate it up and left behind
trails of yellow glistening slime!

Goodbye, you slimy things
I've seen...

I'm glad that you were all a dream!

First published in Great Britain by
Jonathan Cape in 1985
First published in Picture Lions in 1987
This edition published in 1992
Picture Lions is an imprint of the
Children's Division,
part of HarperCollins Publishers Limited,
77-85 Fulham Palace Road, Hammersmith,
London W6 8JB

Printed in Great Britain